Mindfulness and Resilience Skills

for Teens and Kids

For Caregivers

1. It can be difficult for caregivers to know how to respond when they see their child avoiding important situations, acting out frequently, or experiencing intense distress. This workbook is designed to support both you and your child in managing their OCD more effectively.

2. OCD is a highly treatable condition. The methods presented in this workbook are rooted in exposure and ritual prevention (EX/RP) therapy, which is the leading treatment approach for children with OCD.

3. We recommend reviewing the material in this book before working through it with your child. Since OCD can sometimes involve sensitive topics, ensure that each activity is appropriate for your child's specific needs.

For Caregivers Cont.

4. While this book can be a helpful complement to EX/RP therapy, it is not a substitute for professional treatment. If your child's OCD significantly impacts their ability to function at home, school, or in social settings, seeking professional help may be necessary.

5. We sincerely hope that this workbook will aid both you and your child in gaining a better understanding of OCD and managing its symptoms more effectively.

6. In addition, this workbook includes supplementary materials that take a holistic approach, covering topics such as recognizing emotions, grounding and coping techniques, journal prompts, and more.

What is OCD?

1 in 50

individuals
are affected

What is OCD?

OCD functions like a trap. It makes you feel uncomfortable and convinces you that the only way to feel relief is by following its strict rules. These rules can be very precise, but the truth is, they don't really help.

What OCD wants you to think:

What REALLY happens:

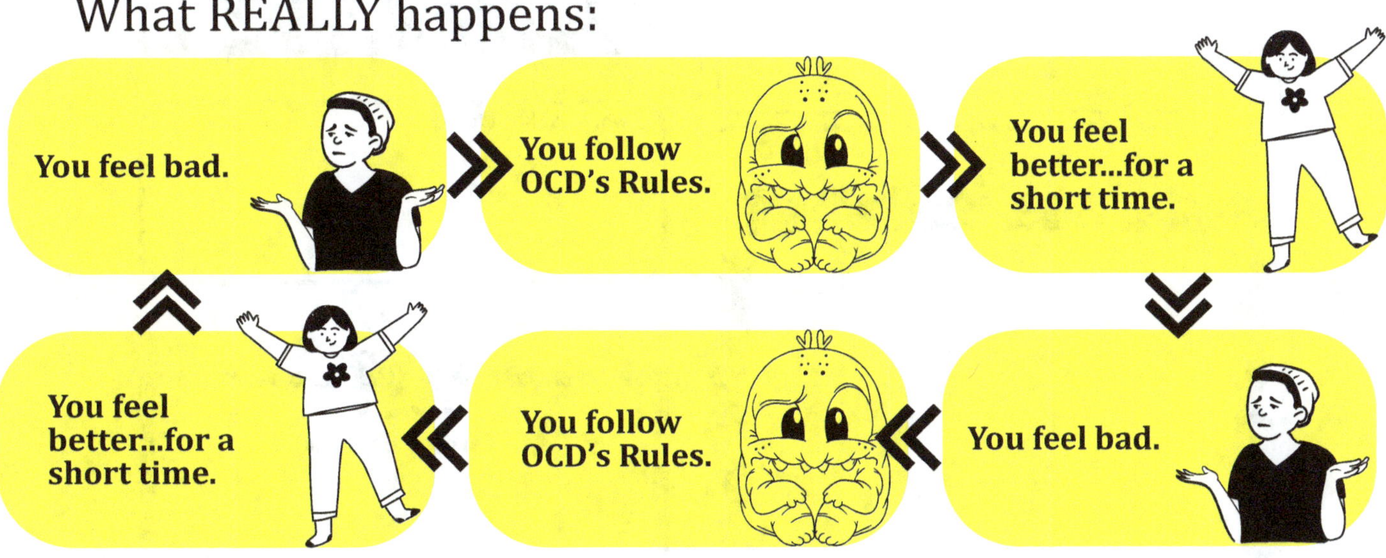

And this cycle just keeps repeating, doesn't it? Does this sound familiar? Do you often feel stuck because of OCD?

This book is here to help you break free from OCD's trap.
But before we dive deeper into OCD, let's focus on you! After all, there's so much more to you than just OCD!

All About Me

Teens can sometimes lose sight of all the amazing aspects of their lives when dealing with OCD. This book is here to help you become stronger than OCD, so it doesn't take over the rest of your life. Use this page to fill in with words and pictures that represent the other important parts of your life.

Why I Want to be
Empowered Over OCD

Gaining empowered over OCD can be challenging at times. Many teens find it helpful to remind themselves why they want to overcome OCD and become stronger.

Below, write at least three reasons why you want to get stronger than OCD. You can use the reasons from a boy named Alex as a guide:

1. OCD makes my nighttime routine long and frustrating.

2. I want to spend time with my friends without having to follow OCD's rules.

3. OCD makes it difficult for me to meet and connect with new people.

Why I want to be empowered over OCD

Regular Thoughts vs.
Sticky Thoughts

Have you ever had a song stuck in your head that you just couldn't stop humming? It can be really annoying, but it's something that happens to everyone. For people with OCD, though, thoughts can be even harder to shake off—they stick around longer and feel more intense. These thoughts often make teens feel anxious or worried that something bad might happen, or that they're not normal. We call these "sticky thoughts," but the official term is "obsessions." Remember how we talked about OCD being like a trap? Trying to quickly get rid of these sticky thoughts is what pulls us deeper into that trap!

Regular Thoughts	Sticky Thoughts
Come and go quickly	Stay around for long periods of time.
Might make you feel concerned, but you can feel better easily.	Make you feel scared or grossed out, and cannot feel better easily.
Rarely return if you don't want them.	Keep coming back.
Can be about anything.	Usually about things you don't like to think about.
Usually come and go on their own; you don't feel you need to do anything to make them go away.	Make you feel like you need to do something to make them go away.

Thoughts	Regular (R) Or Sticky (S)
Kyle wonders what he is having for dinner and then completes his chores.	
Beth thinks, There might be a fire in my house, during class, and has trouble focusing on the activity.	
Maggie imagines hurting her dog, even though she loves him and wouldn't want anything bad to happen to him.	

Understanding My
Sticky Thoughts

Sticky thoughts are a big part of OCD. These are the unwanted thoughts or mental images that pop into your head, which you really don't like. They often make teens feel uneasy or anxious, as if something bad might happen or that there's something wrong with them.

Here are some examples of sticky thoughts that kids have:

Sometimes sticky thoughts feel more like a bad or not-right feeling that you don't like.

Or they are like images or pictures in your head that you don't like.

Understanding My
Sticky Thoughts

Sticky thoughts can be about all kinds of different things. Some kids might have just one or two that really bother them, while others may deal with a bunch of them. Now, take a moment to write down the sticky thoughts that really bother you the most.

Sticky Thoughts That Bother Me a Lot

Beat Sticky Thoughts

When we have painful unwanted thoughts, t is natural to push them away. However, kids and grown-ups are not very good at not thinking of something.

Give it a try:

For the next 30 seconds, try not to think about a blue shark.

Count how many times you thought of a blue shark.

You probably found it is quite difficult.

When we try to avoid thinking about a sticky thought, it actually makes us think about it even more. And the problem is, we're more likely to think about it again later, even after we've tried to stop!

And guess what, you are stuck in OCD's trap!

What to do instead?

Identify the thought as sticky. "It's not what I want to do or believe."

Don't fight with it. If you have an sticky thought, don't try to "make it go away."

Don't be hard on yourself. Having weird or unsettling thoughts doesn't mean there's anything wrong with you.

What Are Compulsions?

You've just learned about one major part of OCD: those frustrating sticky thoughts. The other major part is feeling like you have to follow all the rules that OCD gives you. Kids often feel the need to follow these OCD rules again and again. The actions you repeat to follow these rules are called compulsions.

Common Compulsions Checklist

Place a check mark next to the ones that sound like you.

- [ ] I wash my hands, shower, or clean my stuff a lot.
- [ ] I check to make sure things are safe.
- [ ] I ask my parents a lot of questions to make sure we are safe.
- [ ] I read things over and over.
- [ ] I write things over and over until they look perfect.
- [ ] I save stuff that I may need later even if other people think it's garbage.
- [ ] I repeat my prayers over and over or say prayers a lot.
- [ ] I check in with people a lot to make sure they are not angry with me.
- [ ] I think a lot about how I acted to make sure I did not do something wrong.
- [ ] I need to keep my things arranged in a certain way.
- [ ] I repeat some things I do until it feels "right."
- [ ] I ask my parents the same questions over and over.
- [ ] I think or say "good" words or phrases to cancel out "bad" words or phrases.

What Are Compulsions?

Compulsions can be really frustrating and take up a lot of time. Want to know something important about them? They don't actually work! Think about it—if compulsions really worked, why would you need to do them again and again?

Looking back at the checklist, write down the compulsions that bother you the most.

Compulsions that Bother You

____

____

____

____

____

____

____

____

____

____

Why OCD's Rules Don't Work!

Think about the rules OCD tells you to follow. These might include doing the compulsions you listed in activity 4 or avoiding certain places or people. Now it's time to see if these rules are really helping you. Here's an example from a boy named Ethan.

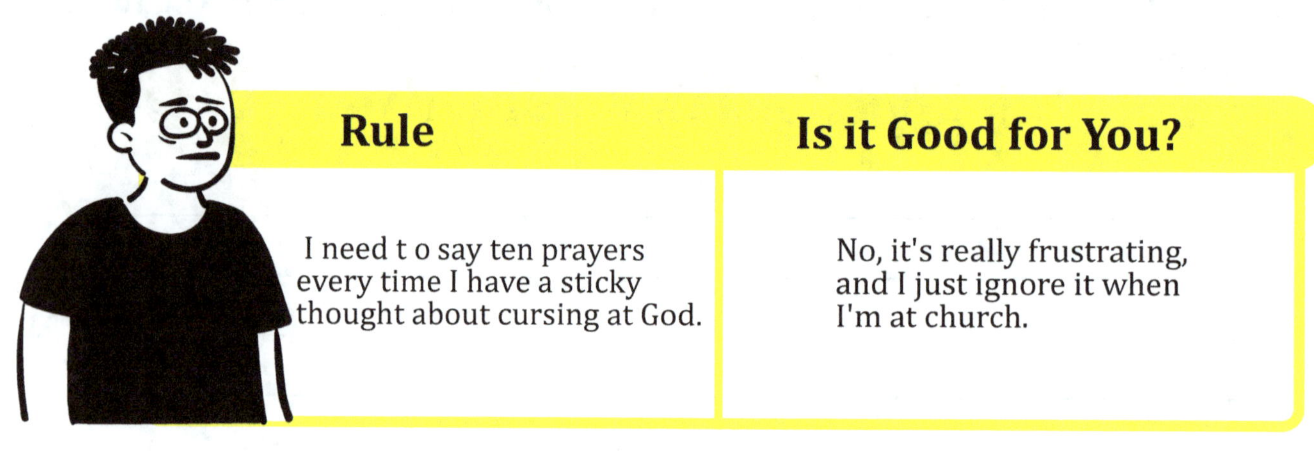

Rule	Is it Good for You?
I need t o say ten prayers every time I have a sticky thought about cursing at God.	No, it's really frustrating, and I just ignore it when I'm at church.

Now list some of your OCD rules and decide if these rules are good for you or not:

Rule	Is it Good for You?

Sticky Thoughts
JOURNAL

**What happened?
(situation or trigger):**

____

____

____

____

____

____

____

**What did you feel about the
thought or impulse? How
intense was the feeling?
(0-10):**

**What unwanted thought
or impulse did you have?
("sticky thought"):**

**What have you done
to deal with this sticky
thought?
Have you practiced
not to fight this thought?**

____

____

____

____

____

____

____

How Does OCD Affect Your Life?

Take a moment to reflect on how OCD impacts various parts of your life. In the table, write down the ways OCD has caused problems for you in these different areas.

Life Area	Is OCD affecting this part of your life? If it is, how does it impact you?
School	
Friendships	
Family	
Sleep	
Healthy eating	
How You Feel	
Hobbies	
Ot her: _______	

Life Without Following OCD's Rules

It can feel overwhelming when OCD affects so many areas of your life. Take a moment to close your eyes and picture what your life would be like if you didn't have to follow OCD's rules. In the space below, write or draw what your life would look like without OCD getting in the way.

What is Your OCD's Name?

Sometimes it can feel like your entire life revolves around managing OCD! But learning to see OCD as something you're dealing with, rather than a part of who you are, can help you become stronger than it.

One way to do this is by giving your OCD a name. Dr. John March suggested that naming OCD helps teens view it as the problem, rather than blaming themselves or their parents (March and Mulle, 1998).

Create a name for your OCD. Here are some examples of names other kids have used for their OCD:

You can choose any name you like for your OCD, but try to pick one that helps you feel stronger and more in control than OCD. In the space below, write down the name you want to call your OCD:

I will call my OCD...

What Does My OCD Look Like

Here is what _________________ looks like:

Who's On Your Team?

Accepting help from others can be tough for many reasons. Some teens might feel a bit embarrassed to ask for help, while others think they should be able to handle things on their own. The good news is, you don't have to face OCD by yourself. At some point, teens realize they need support to manage OCD and reach out to their parents to create a plan and work together as a team.

Here are some ways a team member can support you:

Listen to you when you're having a hard time with OCD
Help you recognize sticky thoughts and OCD's rules
Encourage you to be stronger than OCD and resist compulsions
Assist in planning brave challenges with you (you'll learn more about brave challenges soon)

Take a moment to think about family members, therapists, or teachers you could ask to be part of your support team. These should be people you trust and who are ready to help you along the way.

Write down the names of the people you would like to have on your team, and list the ways they can help support you:

Your Team Members	Ways They Can Help

Consider which aspects of your OCD you feel comfortable sharing with each person on your team. Are you okay with discussing your sticky thoughts and compulsions? You might not want to share everything with every team member, but at least one person should know your OCD as well as you do.

Rating Scale

Sometimes it's difficult to explain just how uncomfortable OCD makes you feel.
Using a rating scale can help you figure out how much OCD is bothering you.
This scale can also help you communicate with your team about how you're feeling.
Think of it like a thermometer: just as the red line goes up when it gets hotter outside,
your rating scale will be higher when OCD feels stronger and you're more
uncomfortable.

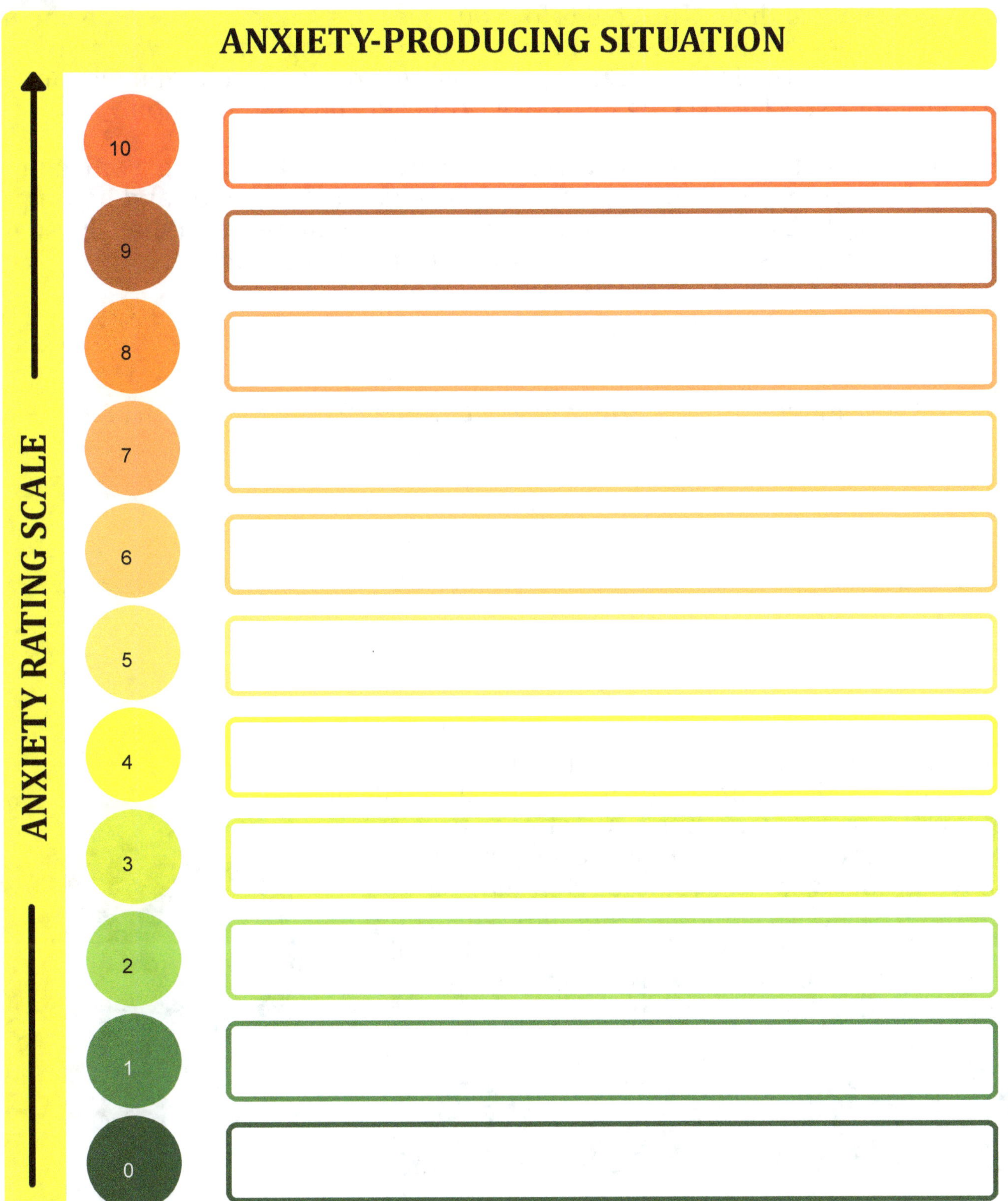

Track Your Compulsions

The next skill we want you to learn is how to become a detective by gathering clues about your OCD! This means paying close attention to your compulsions: when, where, and how often you do them. The goal is for you to learn as much as possible about your compulsions. To help with this, we want you to start keeping track of what you notice—this is called tracking. Tracking your compulsions is simple. You just put a small mark on a special tracking form every time you do a compulsion.

As you track your compulsions, try to spot any patterns that come up. For example, a girl named Rachel had two main compulsions: washing her hands and holding her breath when she thought people around her were sick. She realized that she struggled with these compulsions the most on the days she had swim practice.

Write down two compulsions that you plan to track this week.

1. ____

2. ____

Now, write down the same two compulsions on your tracking form. Each day of the week, pay close attention and put a tally mark every time you notice yourself doing that compulsion. If tracking feels frustrating or annoying, stick with it! Even though it may be bothersome, tracking is helping you build the strength to fight OCD. And remember, if you're having trouble keeping track of your compulsions, don't hesitate to ask a team member for support!

Track Your Compulsions

Day	Compulsion 1: ________________	Compulsion 2: ________________
Sunday		
Monday		
Tuesday		
Wednesday		
Thursday		
Friday		
Saturday		

Standing Up to OCD

Stand-up statements can empower you to become stronger than OCD. What rule does OCD try to make you follow? Use this worksheet to write down the rule OCD gives you, and then write down some statements you can use to remind OCD that you're the one in control.

For example, a boy named Lucas wrote this statement when he got tired of following OCD's rules:

The teacher will let me know if I need to change my answers, not you, Doom-and-Gloom!

OCD's Rule

____

____

My Stand-Up Statement

____

____

____

____

____

Just Notice & Be Present

Remember when we learned that trying to avoid sticky thoughts only makes OCD's trap worse? Instead of trying not to think about them, the best approach is to simply notice the thoughts and stay in the present moment. Write down some things you can say to yourself to help recognize your sticky thoughts and focus on being present.

What to do instead?

Identify the thought as sticky. "It's not what I want to do or believe."

Don't fight with it. If you have an sticky thought, don't try to "make it go away."

Don't judge yourself. Know that having a strange or disturbing thought doesn't mean there is something wrong with you.

Bring your attention back to what you were doing. "I'm drawing a cover for my report. Now I am shading..."

Trying to remember to stay present can be hard, but with practice, it can get easier!

Courageous Challenges & Why We Do Them

You are now ready to learn two important skills that many teens use to beat OCD. These skills are called exposure and ritual prevention, but we'll refer to them as "courageous challenges" and "saying no to compulsions."

A courageous challenge is simple—it means doing something that makes you feel scared, anxious, or uncomfortable. You might be thinking, "That sounds stressful! " Many teens feel the same way. If it were easy, you'd already be doing these challenges. But the good news is that with practice, anything that feels scary or uncomfortable will become less so over time (Jones 1924).

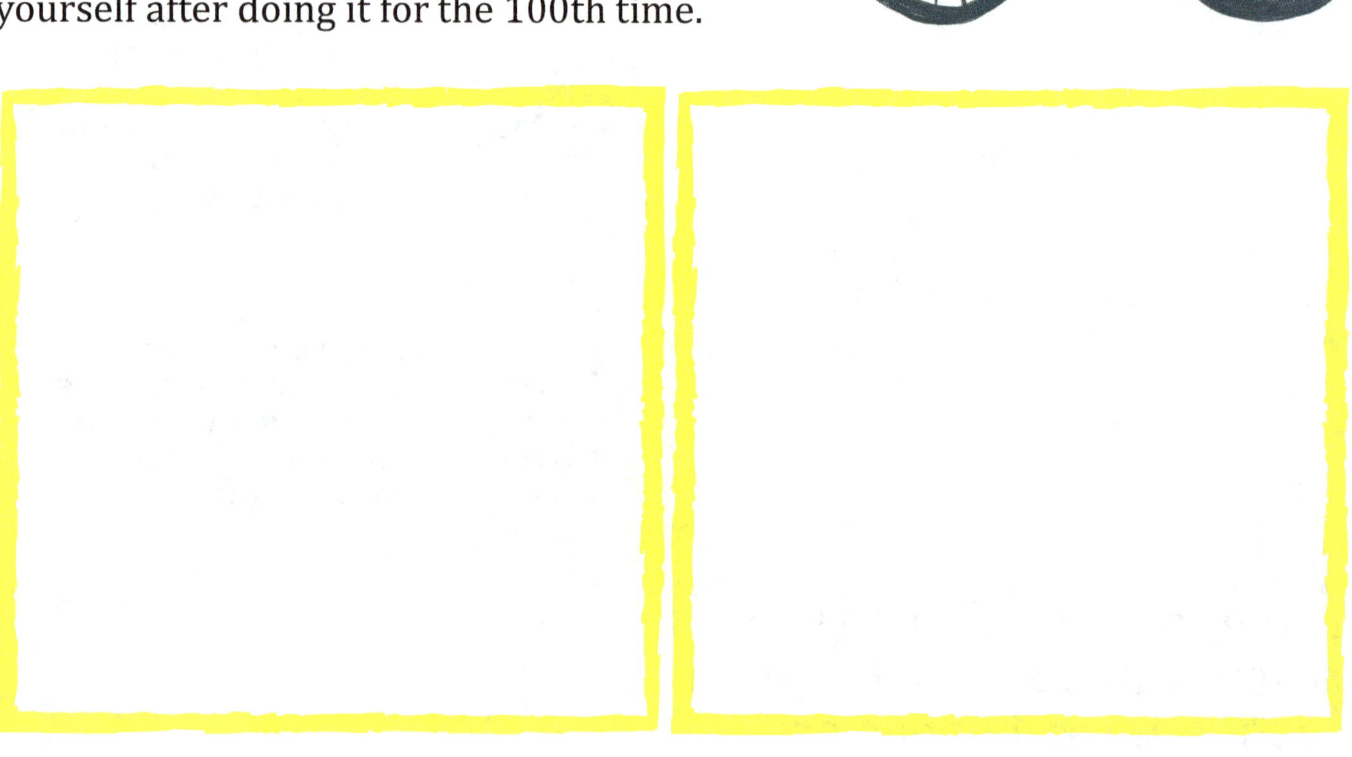

Courageous Challenges & Why We Do Them Think about something that used to scare you but became less frightening the more you did it. Here are a few examples:

Learning to ride a bike
Starting at a new school
Trying a new food

Now, draw a picture of yourself the first time you did something scary, and another picture of yourself after doing it for the 100th time.

Courageous Challenge Ladder

Remember the Rating Scale we talked about earlier? You'll use that as a guide to create your own courageous challenge ladder. It's best to start with easier challenges and work your way up, instead of jumping straight into the toughest one. Once you get more comfortable with the easier challenges, you can take on the harder ones, building confidence as you go until you reach your goal.

At the top of your ladder, write down the challenge that feels the scariest to you, then list others below it that seem easier, until you reach one you think you can handle. Here's an example of a ladder from a girl named Emma.

Challenge	Anxiety Rating
Touch Mom's purse just once and say "This might bring bad luck."	9
Touch all the forks and knives in the kitchen - no tapping at all! Rating	7
Touch the doorknobs all around my house - no tapping at all!	5
Tap my schoolbooks and pencils twice	3
Tap an apple in the supermarket three times and then buy it and eat it	3
Tap an apple in the supermarket three times and leave it there	2

Courageous Challenge Ladder

Say "No" to Compulsions

As you know, when you follow OCD's rules and give in to compulsions, it might make you feel a bit better in the moment, but it also strengthens OCD. Saying no to compulsions might seem tough at first, but it will get easier with practice. Over time, you'll notice that the urge to follow OCD's rules becomes much weaker.

OCD might try to convince you that something bad will happen if you stop doing your compulsions. But remember, that's just an OCD trap!

Think about a compulsion you do to feel safe or to prevent something bad from happening. Now, answer these questions:

Do your family members do that compulsion?

____

Do your friends do that compulsion?

____

Do bad things happen to your friends and family more often than they happen to you?

____

Probably not! That's because compulsions don't protect you from bad things happening. They just make you feel safer for a moment. But once you stop feeling safe, you need to do compulsions again! If your compulsions don't work, why keep doing them? You can start saying no to your compulsions.

Saying "No" Scoreboard

Write down a compulsion that you will practice saying no to.

Today, I will practice saying no to this compulsion: ______________________________

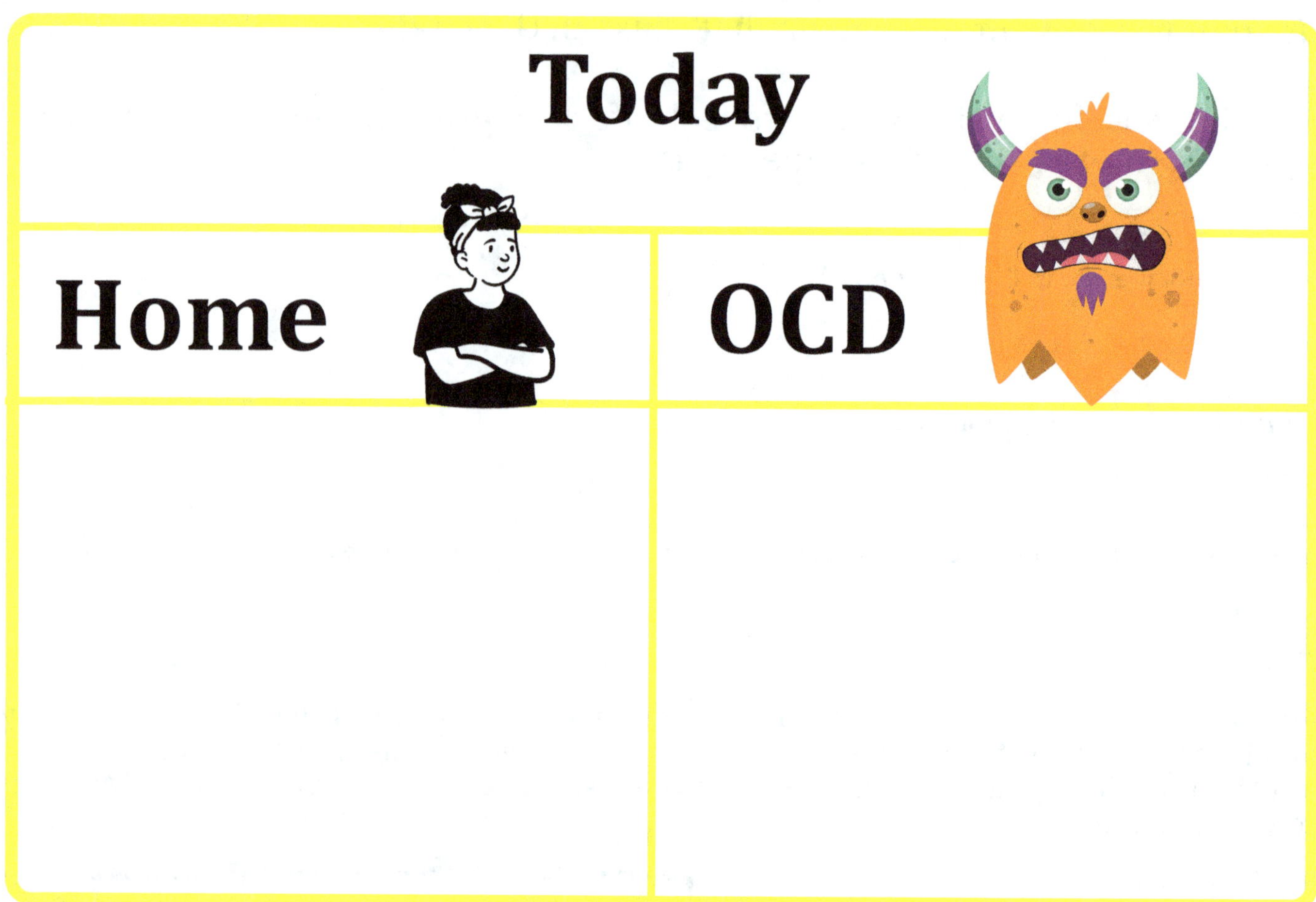

Now, mark your scorecard each time you resist the compulsion and each time you give in to OCD's rule. It might be tough at first, but don't worry! The more you practice, the easier it will get to stop following OCD's rules.

Saying "No" Tracker

Once you feel confident tracking how often you say "no" to compulsions in your daily routine, start using this weekly scorecard. It might be challenging at first, but with continued practice, it will become easier. Don't hesitate to ask your team f or support! Let them know you're standing up to OCD and how they can assist you in the process.

Day	Home Team _______________	OCD's Rule _______________
Sunday		
Monday		
Tuesday		
Wednesday		
Thursday		
Friday		
Saturday		

Courageous Challenge Tracker

Courageous Challenge: _______________________________________

Goal for Courageous Challenge: _______________________________

____

Teammates Who Can Help & How: _______________________________

____

Stand up Statemements: _______________________________________

____

Every time you successfully complete a challenge, mark it in the tracker below.

Sunday	Monday	Tuesday	Wednesday	Thursday	Friday	Saturday

5 Seconds of Bravery

Congratulations! You've built your Courageous Challenge Ladder and made the commitment to say "no" to your compulsions. Now it's time to begin climbing your Courageous Challenge tower. It might seem intimidating, and that's completely normal. Other teens have also felt nervous about taking on their first challenge, but by doing the following exercise, they were able to face their fears and start conquering their towers to defeat OCD!

When you feel too scared to begin a challenge, remind yourself, "I only need 5 seconds of bravery." For example, if one of your challenges is touching a doorknob without washing your hands right after, start by not washing them for just 5 seconds! You don't have to be brave all the time to beat OCD - sometimes, all it takes is 5 seconds of bold courage!

Too Scared to Start?

 **You don't need to be perfect to beat OCD.**

 **You don't need to be brave all of the time to beat OCD.**

 **Just 5 seconds of insane bravery is enough to get started!**

 **Once you see yourself have 5 seconds of bravery, your confidence to tackle your other challenges will increase too!**

Once you start getting comfortable doing 5 seconds of a challenge, try for 6 or 7 seconds next time. Keep increasing the time for each attempt. You can do it! And if you ever feel like it's too much, just go back to a shorter time. Remember, you don't need to perfect, just strive to get better!

Keep Climbing the Ladder!

After practicing courageous challenges for a while, you might notice they're becoming easier! That's great news—it means you're getting stronger than OCD! A girl named Emma noticed her challenges were getting easier too. She and her dad decided to update the ratings next to her challenges. Once she saw her progress, she felt brave enough to take on her hardest challenge.

Challenge	Anxiety Rating	
Touch Mom's purse just once and say "This might bring bad luck."	~~9~~	7
Touch all the forks and knives in the kitchen - no tapping at all! Rating	~~7~~	4
Touch the doorknobs all around my house - no tapping at all!	~~5~~	3
Tap my schoolbooks and pencils twice	~~3~~	1
Tap an apple in the supermarket three times and then buy it and eat it	~~3~~	1
Tap an apple in the supermarket three times and leave it there	~~2~~	1

Take a moment to review your Courageous Challenge Ladder and the ratings you gave each challenge. Would you rate them the same today? Which challenges are starting to feel easier? Update the ratings for any challenges that feel less difficult now. Then, pick one challenge from the ladder that you never thought you'd be ready to face. Work with your team to create a plan to tackle this challenge!

Courageous Challenge Examples
Exposure Ideas : Contamination

Sticky Thoughts About	Challenge Example
Having germs on you	• Touch something sticky like honey or glue and set a timer for a certain amount of time that you agree to not wash your hands. • Go around your house touching "dirty" or "germy" things without washing your hands. • Rinse your hands with water only, and do not use soap.
Feeling Dirty	• Sit in a "dirty" place and play a game. • Walk barefoot in "dirty" places. • Play on a playground that has "dirty" stuff near it, and then have a snack.
A friend or family member being sick or "dirty"	• Have this person make you a snack. • Give this person a hug or shake hands with this person. • Touch this person's clothing. • Have lunch with this person. • Watch TV while sitting next to this person.

Courageous Challenge Examples
Exposure Ideas : Safety

Sticky Thoughts About	Challenge Example
Your house door being unlocked	• Spend some time in your home with the door unlocked (if an adult is home and agrees to this plan). • Have an adult quickly lock the front door without the adult looking before leaving the house. • Read stories or watch movies about burglars robbing homes. Have your parents help you choose one.
Your oven being left on	• Cook or bake with an adult and have the adult be in charge of turning off the oven. • Have an adult quickly turn the stove or oven on and off before leaving the house.
Accidentally poisoning someone	• Make food for your family once a day for a week. • Prepare food for someone and have a spray cleaner nearby on the counter. • Serve food that is expired by one or two days to an adult.
Starting a fire in your house	• Have an adult light some candles in the house; have the adult be in charge of blowing the candles out.

Courageous Challenge Examples

Exposure Ideas : Perfectionism

Sticky Thoughts About	Challenge Example
Doing your homework perfectly	• Make a mistake on a homework assignment on purpose. • Leave a homework question blank. • Give yourself a time limit to complete a homework assignment, and do not go over the time limit.
Writing letters perfectly	• Include a sentence full of messy letters on a homework assignment. • Display a sign with messy handwriting on your bedroom door, refrigerator, or school desk. • Write with the hand you normally do not use for writing.
Making sure your clothes and hair look perfect	• Wear your hair very messy or out of style. • Wear mismatching clothes. • Place a stain on your clothes and go out in public.
Making sure you read something completely	• Speed- read through a favorite book or website. • Skip one sentence on every page or every paragraph.

Courageous Challenge Examples

Exposure Ideas : " Bad " Thoughts

Sticky Thoughts About	Challenge Example
Hurting a family member	• Sit or stand near that family member for fifteen minutes. • Gently place your hands on an adult and keep them there for a minute.
Causing a horrible thing to happen	• Wish over and over that the horrible thing happens (I wish that my grandpa dies or I wish that there is a tornado in Oklahoma). • Write "I hope that ___happens" twenty times in a row (filling in the blank).
Stealing something from a store	• Stealing something from a store
Saying curse words out loud	• Whisper or silently say curse words in public. • Say curse words out loud at home with family members. • Play curse- word Hangman.
Going to Hell	• Read Bible stories describing hell. • Complete a word search with words related to hell. • Say prayers incorrectly

Courageous Challenge Examples

Exposure Ideas : "Not Right"

Sticky Thoughts About	Challenge Example
Your clothes, toys, or other things being out of order	• Place your stuff in the wrong order when you go to school or before you leave the house. • Place one thing out of order and plan to keep it there for at least a week. • Ask a team member to move your stuff out of order without telling you. You are not allowed to rearrange things your team member messes up!
Needing to touch or tap something over and over until it feels "right"	• Pick a time each day when you practice touching something only once. Try to extend this time every few days! • Play a game in which a team member gives you a point every time you touch objects the first time and resist retouching or tapping it. Ten points earns you a reward!
Needing to do something an even number of times	• Play the Odd Olympics! Create a series of tasks you will practice doing an odd number of times. Take an odd number of bites of food, take an odd number of steps before stopping, or blink an odd number of times. (vice versa if your sticky thoughts tell you to do something an odd number of times).

My Progress

____

____

____

____

____

____

What brave challenges are you especially proud of completing? Write them down:

____

____

Say no to all compulsions and look out for new compulsions! Write down the compulsions that you do not do as much anymore:

____

____

You are stronger than OCD!
Keep up the great work!

When OCD Follows You to School

Many teens find that their OCD follows them to school, making it hard to focus, stay seated, or finish work on time. Talking to your teacher or school counselor about your OCD might help, but it's a good idea to discuss it with your parents or caregivers first. If you do talk to your teacher or counselor, they could help you with courageous challenges, support you in saying no to compulsions, and even reward you for standing up to OCD.

Is OCD showing up at school for you too? If it is, talk to your parents about what you'd like your teacher to understand about OCD and come up with a plan together. Write down what you want your teacher to know about your OCD.

Hi ____

____

____

____

____

____

____

____

____

My Progress

Are you finding it hard to complete your brave challenges and say no to compulsions? If so, try to figure out what might be holding you back. Here's a list of common obstacles that can make it difficult to fight OCD. Circle the ones that apply to you, and if you can think of other challenges, add them to the list.

Problems that make it hard to stand up to OCD

I don't want to work on OCD right now. _______________________

I don't feel ready to work on OCD. _______________________

I don't have enough time to work on OCD. _______________________

My team is not available to work on OCD. _______________________

____

____

____

Sit down with members of your team and review the problems that you circled. Come up with solutions to help solve these problems!

Solutions

____

____

____

____

Staying Strong!

Taking on OCD can be really tough, and many teens find it tiring, making it hard to stay energized throughout the day. Just like a car needs fuel to run, we need to refuel our bodies to stay strong and keep fighting OCD!

Here are some ways to recharge your body and mind to stay sharp and get stronger than OCD. Pick two or three that you can start today. Once you decide how to refuel, ask a teammate to help you make a plan. By making these changes, you'll have more energy t o stand up to OCD. It might be challenging at first, but the more you stick with it, the easier it will become!

Better Sleep

Regular Exercise

Eat Healthier

How can you get better sleep each night?

How can you get more exercise during the week?

What can you eat less/more of to have a healthier diet?

I can improve my sleep by: ____

I can eat healthy by: ____

I can stay active by: ____

Who can help me stay accountable to my goals? ____

Caregivers Guide to Courageous Challenges

Do	Do Not
Be honest with your child about what you are willing to do and what challenge involves.	Lie to your child. ("I promise you that I washed my hands twice before I made your sandwich.")
Remind your child that challenges evoke anxiety.	Let your child avoid situations that make her nervous.
Help your child break down Daunting tasks into more manageable ones.	Tell your child that he must do every challenge as written.
Be flexible with the courageous-Challenge plan.	Minimize the child's anxiety. ("There is nothing to be nervous about.")
Remind your child there is always uncertainty and we must learn to face our fears.	Tell your child that you are not responsible for helping with his OCD homework.
Help your child generate new courageous- challenge ideas.	Pretend to not notice the reduction in compulsions for fear of calling too much attention to your child's OCD.
Encourage your child to complete an unplanned challenge when it occurs.	Tell your child she doesn't have to do an unplanned challenge.
Praise or reward your child for the completion of challenges.	
Keep completing challenges until OCD is no longer present.	Take vacations from completing challenges because your child needs a break from working so hard on OCD.
Stay calm, even when your child is resistant to working on courageous challenges.	Reassure your child that everything will be okay and nothing bad will happen if she does a brave challenge.

CALM YOURSELF WITH A
5 FINGER BREATHING
5 BRAIN BREAK

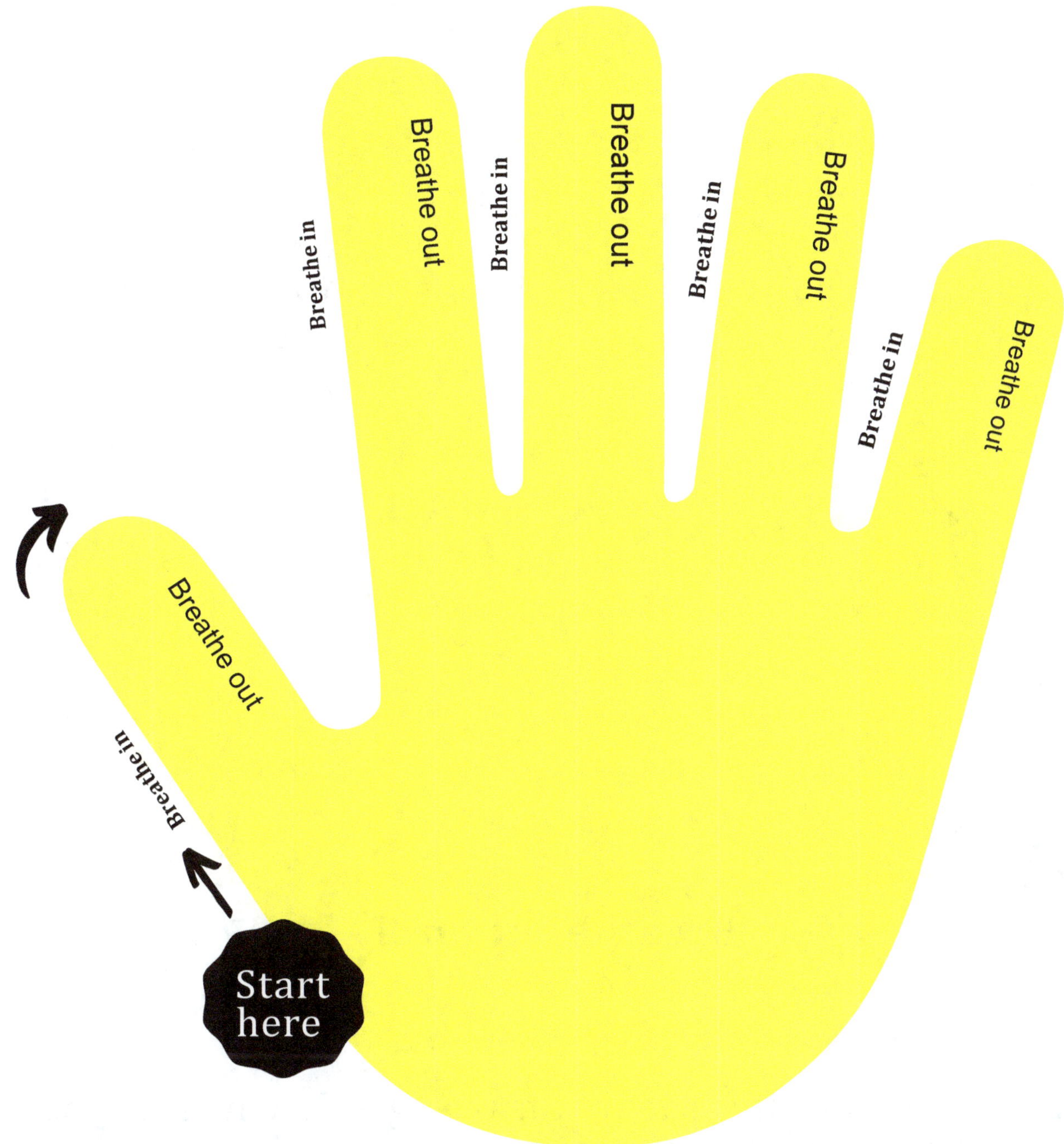

Slowly trace the outside of the hand with the index finger, breathing in when you trace up a finger and breathing out when you trace down. You can also do this breathing exercise using your own hand.

CALM YOURSELF WITH A **TRIANGLE BREATHING** BRAIN BREAK

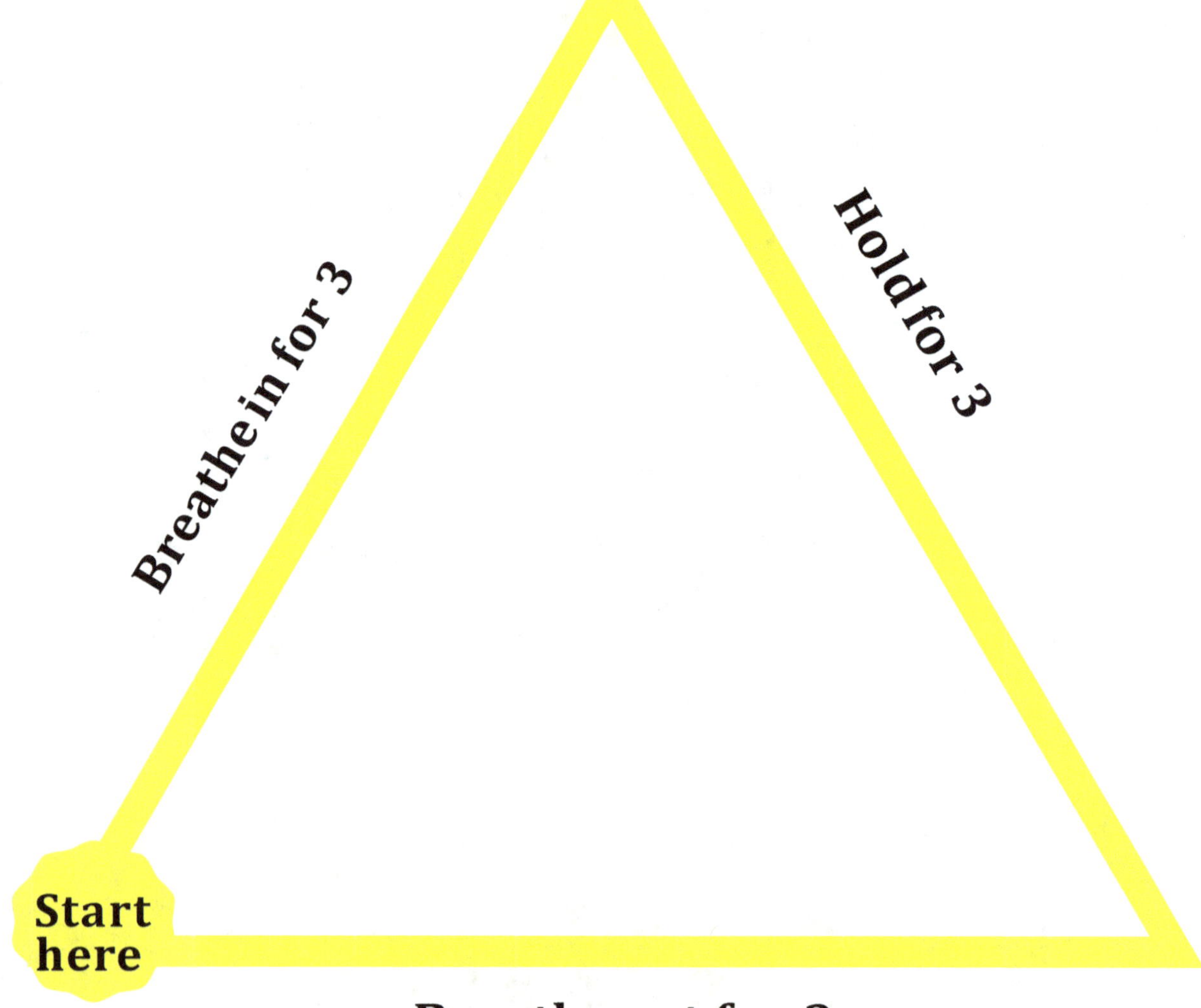

Start at the bottom left corner of the triangle. Slowly trace your finger up one side while taking a deep breath in. When you reach the top, hold your breath for three seconds as you slide your finger down the other side. Finally, breathe out as you move your finger along the bottom of the triangle. Repeat this process until you feel calm.

CALM YOURSELF WITH A
SQUARE BREATHING
BRAIN BREAK

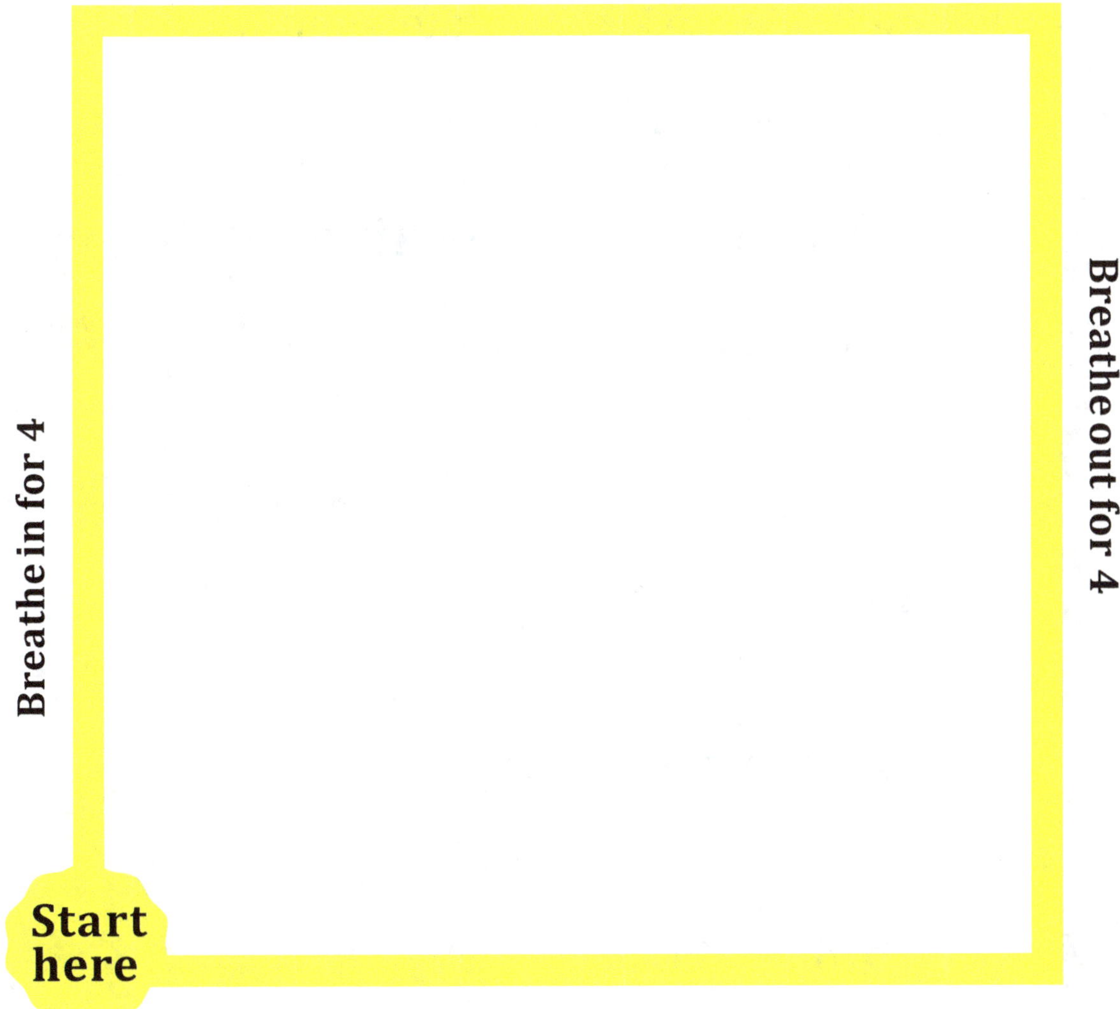

Start at the bottom left corner of the square. Slowly trace your finger up the side while taking a deep breath in. Hold your breath for four seconds as you trace along the second side. Breathe out as you slide your finger down the third side. Then, hold your breath for four seconds as you trace along the bottom of the square. Repeat as needed.

Mood Thermometer

We often experience different emotions before we get angry and lash out. By noticing the warning signs early and taking steps to calm down, we can prevent anger from building up. Practice recognizing how you're feeling and figure out what actions you can take to bring yourself back to a calm state of mind.

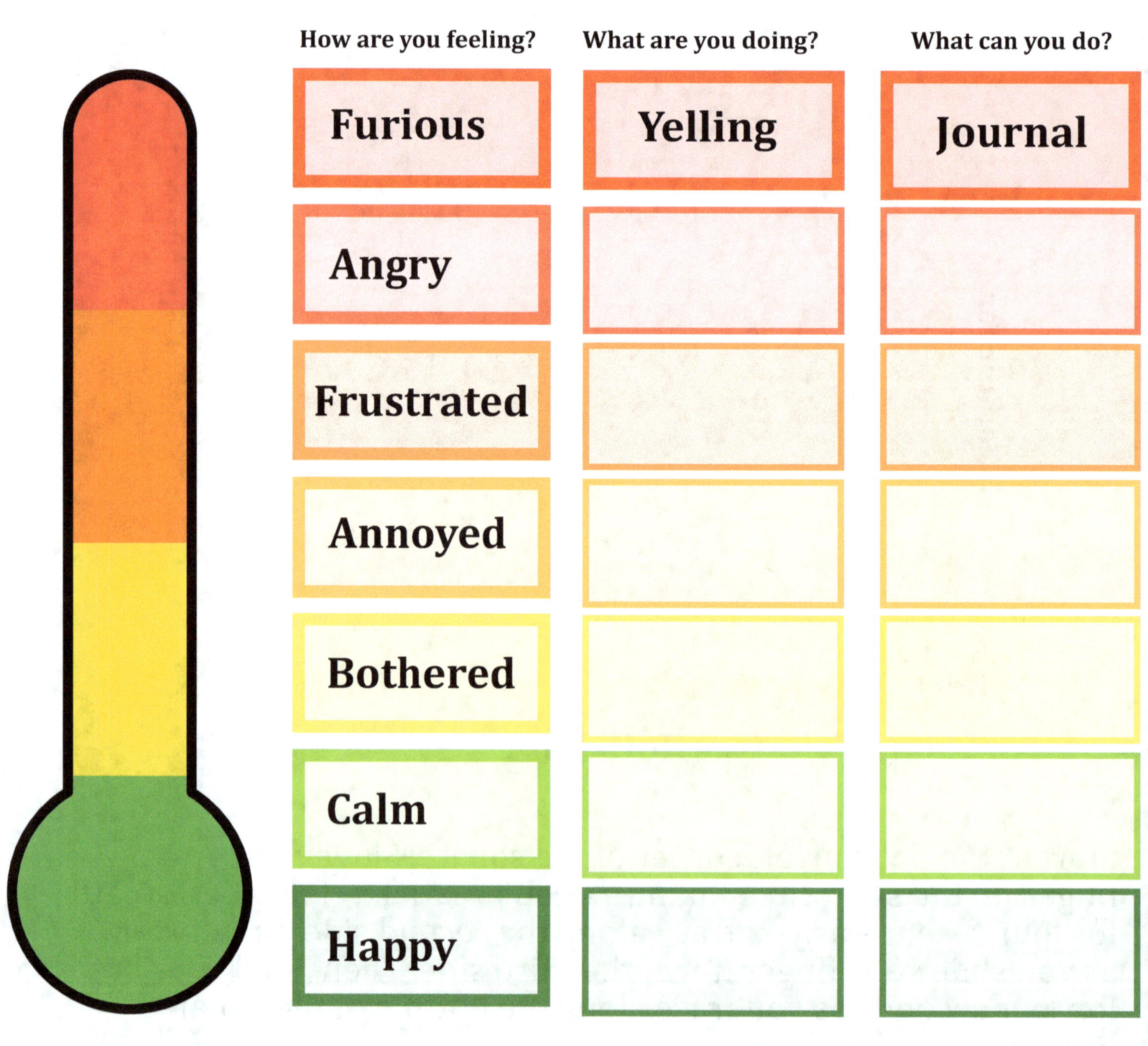

POSITIVE JOURNAL PROMPTS

What qualities make you special? Focus on your strengths and positive traits.

Write a letter to your body, appreciating everything it does for you without any negativity or criticism.

How do you want people to remember you? What actions can you take to leave that legacy?

Make a list of goals or things you'd like to accomplish before the end of this year.

Write down your top three favorite character strengths and why you appreciate them.

List your proudest achievements and see if you can come up with at least 10 moments from different stages of your life.

What's one skill or activity you excel at?

If your best friend were to describe you, what would they say?

What would you do if success was guaranteed and failure wasn't an option?

Who inspires you the most? How are you working to be more like them?

What would your ideal day look like if money wasn't a concern?

If you could master any subject or skill, what would it be and why?

What's your favorite way to spend a quiet afternoon?

POSITIVE JOURNAL PROMPTS

If you could go back and give advice to your younger self, what would it be?

Think about two unforgettable moments in your life—what made them so special?

Write a list of 20 things that make you smile or laugh.

What are your favorite words or a quote that you live by?

How do you show kindness to yourself when you're feeling down?

Write down the names of the people in your life who provide real support and trust.

What does unconditional love mean to you? How do you show it to yourself and others?

What would your life look like if you loved yourself without hesitation? How can you begin practicing this today?

What do you wish more people knew about you?

What's something you are grateful for that you have in your life right now?

If your body could talk, what would it say to you?

Think of a time you showed compassion to someone—how did it feel, and how can you do it again?

What brings you joy about life, even on difficult days?

What always moves you to tears (in a good way)?

What is one area of your life where you can shift your perspective to see things differently?

POSITIVE JOURNAL PROMPTS

What's something that makes you laugh or brings humor into your life?

How can you work on becoming even more grateful each day?

What motivates you to keep going, even during tough times?

What are three things that truly make you feel happy?

How can you show yourself more patience and understanding today?

What is the best compliment you've ever received, and why did it stick with you?

Name a challenge you've overcome and how it made you stronger.

What's something you've learned recently that made a positive impact on your life?

What's your favorite memory, and what makes it so special?

How can you practice being kinder to yourself when you make mistakes?

Write down three things you're proud of about yourself.

How can you bring more positivity into your daily routine?

Think about a time when you made a positive difference in someone's life—what did you do, and how did it feel?

What are three things you're grateful for today that you didn't notice before?

What is one small change you can make today to improve your well-being?

Anxiety In My Body

Rate your week: 1 2 3 4 5   Date: ________________

What was happening when you noticeably felt anxiety this week?

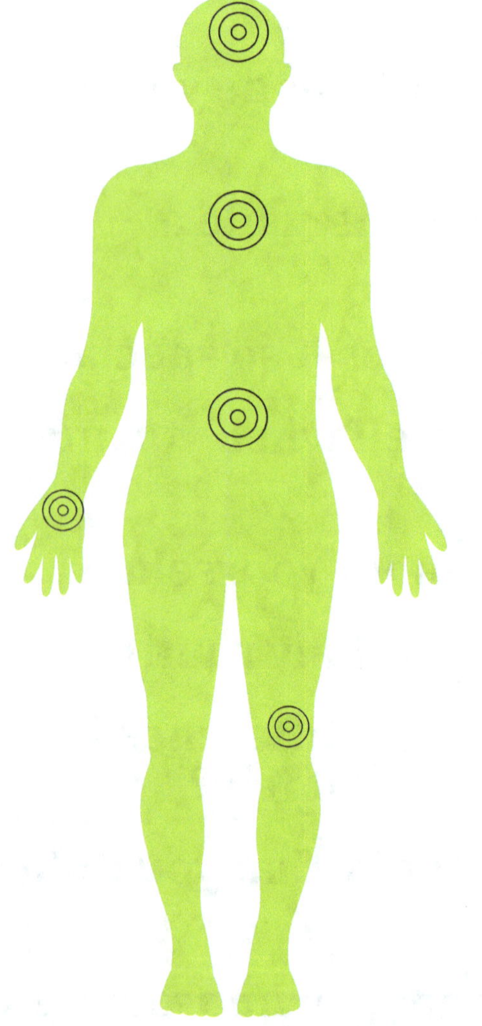

Circle every sensation you've felt in the last week when you were experiencing anxiety.

Headache	**Lightheaded**
Shortness of Breath	**Pounding Heart**
Stomach Pain	**Nausea**
Weakness or Fatigue	**Insomnia**
Sweating	**Trembling**

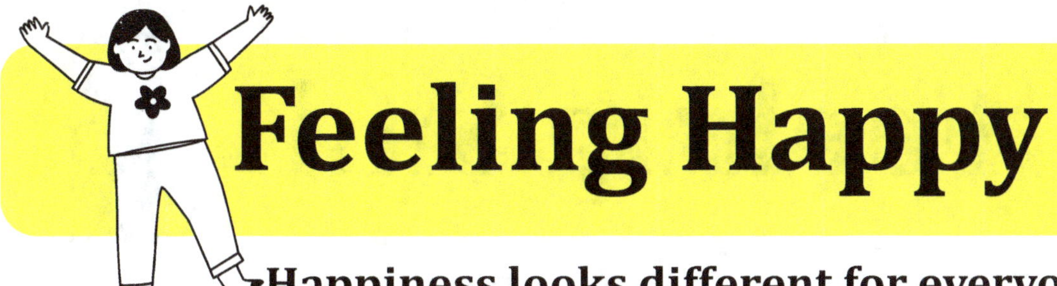

Feeling Happy

Happiness looks different for everyone.

- **What does your face look like when you're happy? Draw it**

- **Write and draw 4 things that make you feel happy.**

- **Write and draw 4 ways in which you express that you are happy.**

Feeling Sad

Sadness looks different for everyone.

- **What does your face look like when you're sad? Draw it**

- **Write and draw 4 things that make you feel sad.**

- **Write and draw 4 ways in which you express that you are sad.**

Feeling Worried

Worry looks different for everyone.

- **What does your face look like when you're worried? Draw it**

- **Write and draw 4 things that make you feel worried.**

- **Write and draw 4 ways in which you express that you are worried.**

Feeling Scared

Fear looks different for everyone.

- Write two synonyms of "scared"

____

- What does your face look like when you're scared? Draw it

- Write and draw 4 things that make you feel scared.

- Write and draw 4 ways in which you express that you are scared.

Feeling Angry

Anger looks different for everyone.

- **What does your face look like when you're angry? Draw it**

- **Write and draw 4 things that make you feel angry.**

- **Write and draw 4 ways in which you express that you are angry.**

List of Emotions

Anger: Resentment, Wrath, Rage, Hostility, Frustration, Aggravation, Annoyance, Irritation

Disgust: Contempt, Loathing, Bitterness, Revulsion, Scorn

Envy: Jealousy, Spite

Fear: Anxiety, Panic, Terror, Apprehension, Uneasiness, Dread, Fright, Alarm

Surprise: Amazement, Astonishment

Love: Affection, Adoration, Compassion, Fondness, Sentimentality, Attraction, Tenderness

Distress: Tenseness, Worry, Nervousness, Mortification

Happiness: Joy, Contentment, Satisfaction, Delight

Anger: Fury, Outrage, Ferocity, Hate, Rage, Hostility, Resentment, Wrath, Grumpiness, Irritation

Disgust: Revulsion, Loathing, Contempt, Spite, Vengefulness, Bitterness, Scorn, Dislike

Fear: Terror, Horror, Panic, Fright, Shock, Alarm, Apprehension, Anxiety, Uneasiness, Hysteria

Surprise: Amazement, Astonishment, Shock, Wonder

Love: Adoration, Affection, Attraction, Compassion, Fondness, Tenderness, Sentimentality, Liking, Infatuation

Distress: Worry, Nervousness, Tenseness, Uneasiness, Torment, Dread

Happiness: Joy, Delight, Satisfaction, Contentment, Euphoria

List of Emotions

Sadness: Sorrow, Grief, Loneliness, Heartache, Despair

Joy: Excitement, Elation, Bliss, Jubilation, Glee, Cheerfulness, Delight, Playfulness

Sadness: Melancholy, Despair, Gloom, Grief, Sorrow, Disappointment, Heartache, Regret

Anger: Annoyance, Frustration, Rage, Wrath, Vexation, Exasperation, Indignation, Fury

Fear: Dread, Unease, Trepidation, Nervousness, Worry, Insecurity, Paranoia, Phobia

Love: Devotion, Infatuation, Passion, Warmth, Compassion, Admiration, Fondness, Affection

Surprise: Bewilderment, Astonishment, Shock, Amazement, Wonder, Startlement

Disgust: Repulsion, Distaste, Aversion, Contempt, Nausea, Offense

Confusion: Perplexity, Uncertainty, Bewilderment, Puzzlement, Hesitation

Trust: Confidence, Reliance, Assurance, Safety, Faith, Certainty

Shame: Embarrassment, Guilt, Humiliation, Mortification, Regret, Remorse

Anticipation: Eagerness, Excitement, Hopefulness, Suspense, Expectation, Optimism

Pride: Satisfaction, Accomplishment, Dignity, Self-respect, Triumph, Esteem

Affirmations

4 Keys to Successful Affirmation Statements:
• It must be believable and within your control
• It must be present tense (happening now), from your perspective (I statements), positive (no "not" or "don't")
• You must FEEL IT when you think it, as if you believe it
• You must repeat it REGULARLY

Negative Thought or Belief	Positive Empowering Belief

Putting Thoughts On Trial

Thought:

Prosecution:
Evidence against the thought

Defense:
Evidence supporting the thought

Verdict:
Is the thought fair or accurate? Is there another possible explanation?:

Realms of Control

Anxiety often arises when we spend too much time focusing on things we can't control, while forgetting about the things we can. Usually, especially in times like these, those things are basic self-care activities like getting enough sleep, staying hydrated, eating well, and moving our bodies. This activity helps us shift our focus back to what we can manage.

The diagram below shows the three areas of control: no control, influence, and control. On the next page, fill out your own circles of control based on this idea.

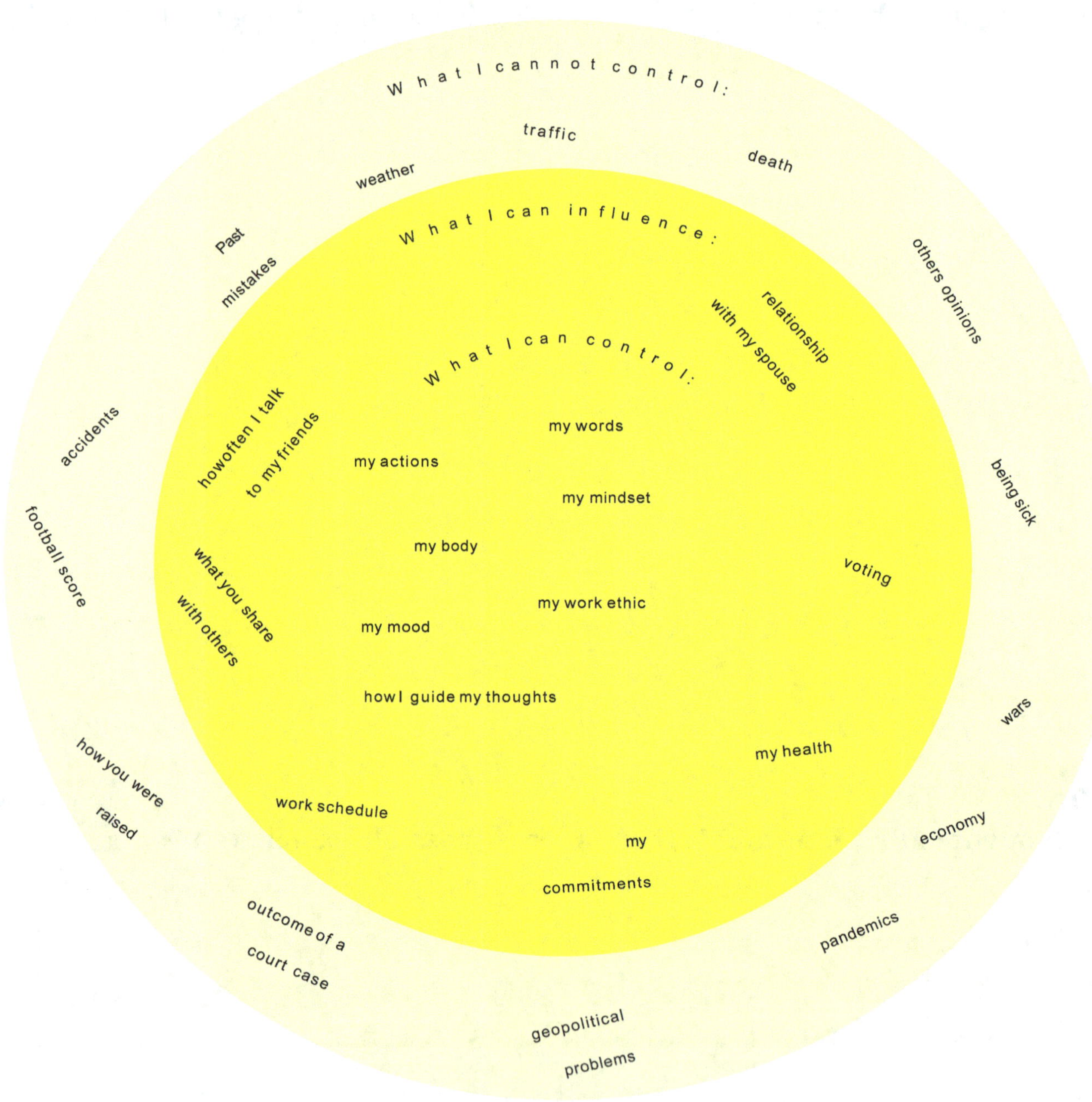

Smart Goals
Setting realistic and achievable outcomes.

My goal is:

S — Specific

What do I want to happen?

M — Measureable

How will I know when I have achieved my goal?

A — Attainable

Is the goal realistic and how will I accomplish it?

R — Relevant

Why is my goal important to me?

T — Timely

What is my deadline for this goal?

Congratulations on Completing Your Journey!

The fact that you've made it this far is a huge accomplishment.

You've taken important steps to better understand your emotions, your thoughts, and yourself — and, most importantly, you've learned real skills to build resilience, confidence, and strength. That is no small feat, and you should feel incredibly proud of your courage and hard work.

Remember, challenges don't define you.

They are just a part of your journey — but they don't control your story. You are stronger than any fear or obstacle, and you've proven that by showing up, learning, and practicing new strategies throughout this guide.

Here are a few important things to keep in mind as you move forward:

🌟 Progress, Not Perfection:

Some days will be easier, some days harder — and that's okay. Every small step you take is a victory worth celebrating.

🌟 You're Not Alone:

Family, friends, teachers, or mentors — your support team is there for you. Asking for help is a sign of strength, not weakness.

 **Celebrate Every Win:**

Whether it's facing a fear, managing a tough moment, or simply having a better day than yesterday, every success matters.

Keep Being Brave:

Courage isn't the absence of fear — it's choosing to move forward even when things feel difficult. You've already proven how brave you are!

And most importantly —

You are so much more than any challenge you face.

Your talents, dreams, passions, and kindness are what truly make you special. With the skills you've developed, you have the power to create a life full of purpose, strength, and joy.

Keep believing in yourself.

Keep practicing.

Keep moving forward.

You've got this!